Forest Tracks

by
Dee Dee Duffy

illustrated by
Janet Marshall

BOYDS MILLS PRESS

Publisher Cataloging-in-Publication Data
Duffy, Dee Dee.
    Forest tracks / by Dee Dee Duffy ; illustrated by Janet Marshall.—1st ed.
[32]p. : col. ill. ; cm.
Summary : The footprints of a woodpecker, rabbit, deer, raccoon, bear, and
skunk are shown along with the animals that made them and the tire
tracks of the forest ranger who lives nearby.
ISBN 1-56397-434-7
1. Animal tracks—Fiction—Juvenile literature. [1. Animal tracks—Fiction.]
I. Marshall, Janet, ill. II. Title.
591.5   [E]—dc20   1996   AC
Library of Congress Catalog Card Number 95-77783

Published by Bell Books
Boyds Mills Press, Inc.
A Highlights Company
815 Church Street
Honesdale, Pennsylvania 18431
Printed in Mexico

First edition, 1996
Book designed by Cathryn Falwell and Janet Marshall
The text of this book is set in 40-point Clarendon light.
The illustrations are done in cut paper.
Distributed by St. Martin's Press

10 9 8 7 6 5 4 3 2 1

To Rick and Regan,
Mom and Dad,
and Jeff and Jenny,
with love
                —D.D.

To Pat Boyle, Amy Ullrich,
and Karen Klockner,
in appreciation
                —J.M.

Look! I see some animal tracks.

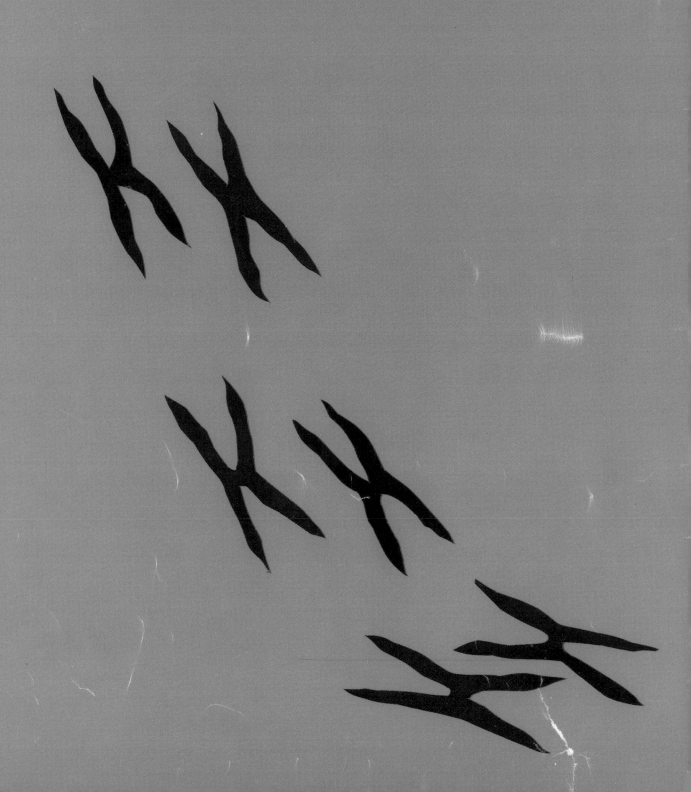

Listen! I hear

rat-a-
tat-
tat

Who's there?

It's the
woodpecker.

Look! I see some animal tracks.

Listen! I hear

thump thump

Who's there?

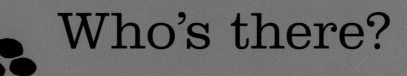

It's the rabbit.

Look! I see some animal tracks.

Listen! I hear

crackle
snap

Who's there?

It's the deer.

Look! I see some animal tracks.

Listen! I hear

Who's there?

It's the raccoon.

Look! I see some animal tracks.

Listen! I hear

grrrr

Who's there?

It's the bear.

Look! I see lots of animal tracks.

what's happening?

It's the skunk!

Look! I see some strange tracks.

What could they be?

Tire tracks!

Even the
forest
ranger
is heading
for home.